First published in Great Britain in 2001.
This edition published in 2006 by Brimax Publishing Ltd
Appledram Barns, Birdham Road, Chichester, PO20 7EQ, UK
© Brimax Publishing Ltd

Printed in China

Ping Won't
Share

BRIMAX

Ping and his friends, Shi Shi and Yang, were
very hungry. The pandas' favorite food was bamboo,
but their supply was running out. They searched the
forest high and low, with their tummies rumbling,
but they couldn't find any more bamboo.
"What will we do if we never find any food?"
cried Shi Shi.

"Let's look one more time," said Yang. "We'll go in separate directions and meet back here later."

Ping trudged through the forest searching for food, but hunger made him tired, so he headed home for a nap. He could not believe his luck when he found a large patch of bamboo growing near his home.

Sitting under a tree, Ping munched his way through a leafy pile of bamboo, then rubbed his full tummy and sighed happily.

This will last me for days, thought Ping.

But I won't tell anyone else what I've found, otherwise they might want to share it, too.

Later, as the sun was going down,
Ping and his friends sat in a circle and shared
their last branch of bamboo. Ping took just a
small bite and left the rest for the others.
"How do you stay so big and strong when you
eat so little, Ping?" asked Yang.
"Oh, I don't need much food," replied Ping,
thinking guiltily of his secret dinner.

When his friends were sound asleep
that night, Ping lay wide awake.
*I am being greedy, keeping all that bamboo
for myself*, thought Ping. He resolved to
share the bamboo with his friends.

But the next morning, when Ping's tummy
rumbled, he quickly changed his mind.
Sneaking away, Ping crept to the pile
of bamboo he had gathered and had
a breakfast feast, all by himself.

Ping's friends sadly decided it was time
to leave their homes and travel
far away in search of food.
"I know where you can find bamboo,"
squawked a nosy pheasant, perched on
a branch. The bird pointed his wing toward
a snow-covered peak in the distance.
"It grows on that mountainside," he said.

When Ping told his friends that he was not
going with them, they looked very sad.
"I am happy here, and I don't need much
food to keep me fit and strong," lied Ping.

Waving goodbye, Yang and Shi Shi
set off on their long journey.
"I hope you find lots of bamboo," called Ping.
As he watched them leave, Ping wished he could have
given his friends just a little bamboo for their trip.
"But if I had, they would have asked where
it came from," said Ping with a sigh.
"And I wouldn't want to share it ALL."

At first, Ping was happy. He had the birds and the butterflies to keep him company, and there was plenty to eat. But as the days passed, Ping's supply of bamboo grew smaller and smaller, until one day there was nothing left. Ping rubbed his rumbling tummy and thought about his friends in their new home.

One afternoon, as Ping searched for tiny scraps
of bamboo, the pheasant swooped down.
"It's a pity you didn't go with your friends,"
chirped the bird. "They found lots
of bamboo and cozy new homes."
"If only I had shared my bamboo,"
whimpered a lonely and hungry Ping.
"I wouldn't be all alone with nothing to eat."

Settling back down in his favorite spot,
Ping remembered how much fun he used
to have playing with Shi Shi and Yang.
He missed their games of hide-and-seek.

Big tears began to roll down his face as
he remembered how badly he had treated
his friends. He was soon sobbing so loudly
that he did not hear two familiar voices
calling out, "Hello, Ping!"

"Don't cry, Ping," said Shi Shi and Yang as they gathered around him. "We've come back to share the bamboo we found." Wiping away his tears, Ping jumped to his feet and hugged his friends.

"I've missed you two so much!" he cried. Ping felt very ashamed of his selfishness and told his friends all about the supply of bamboo he had kept for himself.

Yang and Shi Shi could hardly believe
what they were hearing.
"How could you just let us go hungry?"
demanded Yang angrily.
"You've been very selfish,"
said Shi Shi, shaking her head.

"I am *so* sorry," wailed Ping. "Will you please
forgive me?" He looked very sad and sorry.

Realizing that Ping had truly learned his lesson,
his friends forgave him. They shared some of their
bamboo with Ping, for he would need
strength for the journey ahead.
"From now on, we'll always stick together," said Shi Shi.
"From now on, I'll always share with
my friends," promised Ping.
Munching their bamboo happily, the three
pandas watched the sun set together.

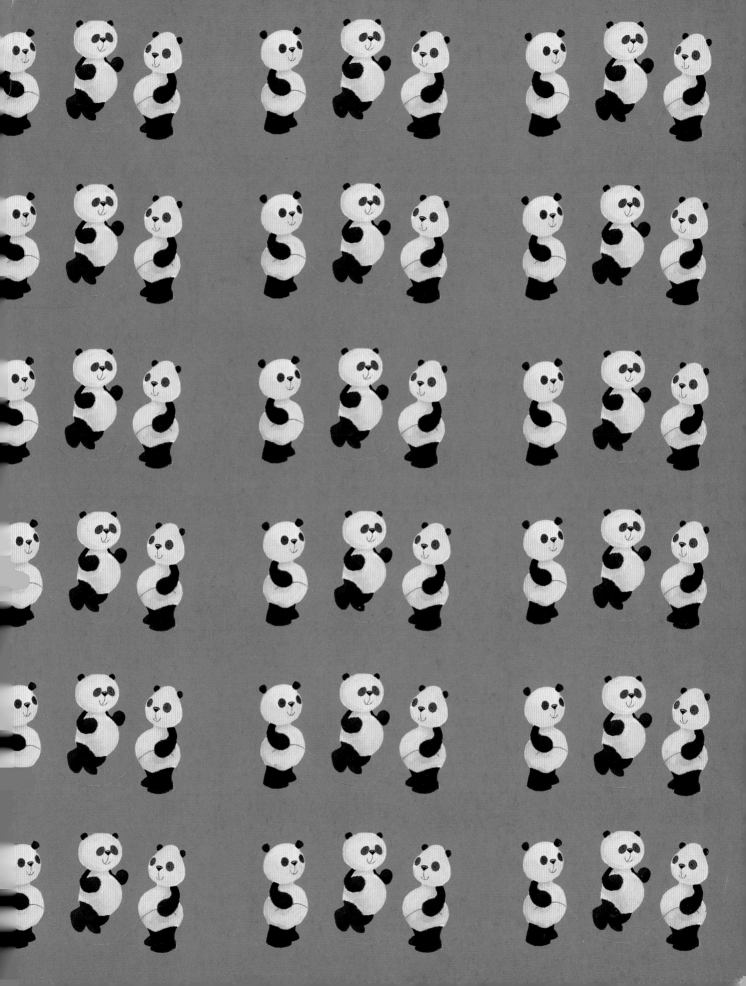